Mabel Lucie Attwell's
Going-to-Bed Tales

Mabel Lucie Attwell's
Going-to-Bed Tales

Michael O'Mara Books Limited

First published in Great Britain in 1994 by
Michael O'Mara Books Limited
9 Lion Yard
Tremadoc Road
London SW4 7NQ

A CIP catalogue record for this book is available from the
British Library

ISBN 1-85479-938-X

New stories and poems by Anne Forsyth
Designed by Mick Keates

Typeset by Florencetype Ltd, Kewstoke, Avon
Printed and bound in Singapore by Toppan Printing Co

Contents

Sleepyhead

Early today I'm sure I heard
On the window-sill, a little bird.
It sang, 'Wake up, you sleepyhead!
It's far too late to lie in bed!'

BUNTY AND THE LITTLE BOOS

It was the Green Umbrella's doing really, for if it had not suddenly turned inside out and flown away over the sea, carrying Bunty, Mops and Queen Elizabeth the doll with it, they would never have found the Little Boos. That's quite certain!

The Brown Rabbit helped a little, for if it hadn't called 'Stop!' just when it did, they might have flown on and on, and there is no knowing what might have happened. I do know that they were all very relieved when – bump, bumpity-bump – they were on firm land once more. Especially Mops – he is the dog.

They all picked themselves up, and Bunty saw a quaint little creature hurrying along. 'Oh, please!' cried Bunty politely, 'are we going right? We have lost our way.'

'Yes,' said the mouse (for that is what the creature was) 'straight on. I've given notice,' she continued.

Bunty was very interested. 'Notice?' she said. 'Are you a cook?'

'Yes, I'm a cook.' The quaint creature shook its whiskers angrily, 'but they get no more cooking from me! They said everything I made tasted of cheese – just cheese – so of course I gave notice at once!'

'What an unpleasant person,' thought Bunty, as the mouse hurried away. 'But I wonder who she gave notice to, and where we are, and who lives in these little houses.'

As they were all tired, they climbed on to a comfort-able tree to rest, but hardly were they seated when a squeaky voice asked for their tickets.

'What tickets?' cried Bunty, who certainly hadn't any – not even halves.

'Tickets for the Little Boos concert tonight,' went on the voice, 'and if you haven't any, you must come along with me to the King.'

Bunty looked around and there, just beneath them, was a little man anyone could see was a policeman. So they simply had to go although Mops *did* make rather a fuss. (Bad dog.)

The King, directly he saw Bunty, loved her dearly, and tried to think how he could have her always, for keeps.

'I know – you are the new cook!' he cried suddenly.

'Am I? How perfectly lovely!' said Bunty.

'*Can* you cook?' he asked a little anxiously.

Bunty shook her head. 'Only mud pies,' she said humbly.

'Despatch a messenger to the Wise Bird,' ordered the King. 'She will lend us the Blue Book of Cooking. Bunty shall learn to make porridge.'

'Hurrah!' shouted all the Little Boos. 'Hurrah for Bunty, the Little Boos' cook!'

There was great excitement! So a Little Boo messenger (quick lad) flew off at once to the Wise Bird's house. The Wise Bird was about to bath her grandchildren but she most kindly hurried to find the book.

'To make porridge, eh?' she said, on hearing the Little Boo's tale. 'Yes! Yes! Easy enough,' she continued, wisely wagging her beak, 'stir sixteen and a half times and boil till the moon rises. Not a minute more, mind you, or the porridge will be spoilt.'

The Little Boo gratefully thanked her and flew quickly homewards, anxious to be in good time to allow Bunty to do her cooking before going to the concert.

The King and Bunty were great friends, he graciously helping the little cook with her task. 'Fourteen, fifteen, sixteen stirs,' he counted.

'Dear me,' thought Bunty, 'this is a great responsibility, and how can one stir a half times?' The porridge was soon made and put on to boil, and the King, Cook and all the Little Boos went to the concert.

When they came to the concert place, Bunty was rather perplexed as to what to sit on. You see, her mother had always said, 'Never, never sit on the grass or the damp will get your bones' and there was nothing else to sit on!

The Little Boos had nice comfortable mushroom seats, but Bunty was too big for them and broke every one she tried to sit on! Hard luck! So once again the King despatched his men, this time for a seat for Bunty. And wasn't it hard work to drag it along! But it was done.

The concert was an enormous success and everybody enjoyed themselves greatly, till Bunty suddenly caught sight of the moon.

It had more than risen, indeed it was half way up the tree. 'Oh dear, my poor porridge!' cried Bunty, as she remembered the Wise Bird's words, 'Sixteen and a half times and boil till the moon rises.'

She hurried away, but too late – the porridge was quite spoilt. 'It is burnt!' she sobbed, 'and I can't cook, that's certain.'

The concert came quickly to a close, and the King hurried to Bunty.

'Don't cry,' he begged, 'we are not hungry, are we, Boos? At least, not very.'

One and all the Little Boos agreed with him, and all begged the sad little cook not to cry one tear more.

'Come,' said the King, 'you are tired. Come and I will find a little house for you to sleep in.'

So Bunty dried her eyes and followed him. But more trouble!

Not one house was anything like large enough for Bunty, to say nothing of Mops and Queen Elizabeth. You see, Bunty

was not like the Little Boos, who can get smaller and smaller just as they like and so can fit any house. No, Bunty was – well – plump, and there it was.

But Bunty had a glorious plan. 'Why not all come back to Mother? My mother is the best in all the world, and loves lots of children in her house, and' (here Bunty blushed), 'she can make lovely porridge!'

So the Green Umbrella carried them safely home to Bunty's mother. And she was surprised. And if, in her heart of hearts, she thought there would be a number of little faces to wash, and stockings to mend, and mouths to fill, she said not a word, but opening her arms, took them all in and loved them to their hearts' content.

Sunflowers

I wonder why that sunflower grew
So fine and straight and tall.
I watered mine and weeded too,
They didn't grow at all!

There was a Little Girl

There was a little girl and she had a little curl
Right in the middle of her forehead.
When she was good, she was very, very good
But when she was bad, she was horrid.

WHEN THE CLOCKS STOPPED

'It's going to be a wild night,' said the people who lived in the village by the wood. They closed the doors of their little houses and pulled the curtains.

'Brrr . . .' said the rabbits as they scurried for shelter.

The wind howled and the trees swayed just as if it were autumn instead of summer.

Next morning, the storm had died down. But only the tall pine trees stood unharmed. Most of the flowers had been flattened by the winds.

Thomas the Toffeemaker opened his door and blinked at what he saw.

'You're out and about very early, Mrs Duck,' he called.

'I'm going shopping,' she said.

'You're much too early,' Thomas said. 'The shops won't be open.'

'How should I know the time?' she replied. 'All the dandelion clocks have blown away in the night.'

Everyone in the village told the time by dandelion clocks. You held the dandelion by its stem and puffed, 'One o'clock, two o'clock . . .' until you had blown all the feathery seedlings away.

'There's not a clock in the place,' she said.

'Dear oh dear,' said Thomas. 'Well, I'm only guessing, but I'd say it was about seven o'clock.'

'Well, I'd better go home, then,' said Mrs Duck rather crossly.

All day long, people kept doing things at very odd times. The children didn't know when it was time to go to school. The bus to town arrived much too early and left right away. So it left without the mice and the hedgehogs who had planned a day in town.

Only one person had a proper clock – an alarm clock – and that was the Queen of the wood.

Late that night, when nearly everyone was asleep, she bounced out of her palace. 'Look at this!' she waved her alarm clock angrily. 'It's ringing and ringing and it can't be time to get up. It's still moonlight!'

The ladies-in-waiting woke up and the sentry stood to attention.

None of them liked to say that the Queen had set her clock for twenty-five minutes to twelve instead of seven

o'clock. You can't tell a Queen that she has done some-thing silly.

'Bother!' she said crossly. 'A dandelion clock is much better!' She threw the alarm clock into the bushes, where it went tick-tick-tick, then stopped altogether.

'Bother!' she said, and went back to bed.

So now there were no clocks at all in the village.

One day soon afterwards, a Prince came riding through the wood. He had travelled a long way and he was very tired, so he tied his horse to a tree, sat down to rest, and quickly fell asleep.

He slept for a long time and when he awoke, it was dark.

'Ah!' He rose and stretched and rubbed his eyes. 'I must set off again.' But then he paused. 'Which way should I take?' There were three paths that seemed to lead out of the wood.

'This way, I think,' he said to himself, and he picked up the reins. But the path took him deeper into the wood.

He turned about and tried the second path, then the third, but without success. He still could not find the way out of the wood.

'I'm lost,' he said, and sat down to think what he should do.

But just then he saw something very strange – tiny lights bobbing along the path. 'Who's there?' he called.

'Here we are – we can help you!' Six or seven elves, each carrying a lantern, appeared before him. 'Follow the lights,' said the first elf. 'We'll soon show you the way.'

In no time they had led the Prince out of the wood and set him on the path to the city.

'How can I thank you?' asked the Prince before he rode off. 'You must tell me how I can reward you.'

'I know!' said the second elf. 'We don't have any way of telling the time. All the dandelion clocks have blown away.'

'Then I'll send you a clock,' said the Prince, 'a fine clock to hang on the boughs of the tallest tree in the village.'

A few days later, the Prince's servant arrived in the village, carrying a fine clock. The woodpecker drilled the holes in an oak tree, the carpenter hammered in a nail, and the Queen of the wood handed the clock to two squirrels who scrambled up and hung the clock on the nail.

'Hurray!' everyone shouted. 'Now we can tell the time!'

'Dinner time!' said the wise old owl, and all the creatures of the wood vanished to their homes. 'How would we know it was dinner time without a clock?' they said. 'What a fine gift!'

Ride a Cock-horse

Ride a cock-horse to Banbury Cross,
To see a fine lady upon a white horse.
Rings on her fingers, and bells on her toes,
She shall have music wherever she goes.

Rock-a-bye Baby

Rock-a-bye baby on the tree top,
When the wind blows, the cradle will rock.
When the bough breaks, the cradle will fall
And down will come baby, cradle and all.

JOSIE'S SECRET

Josie just couldn't keep a secret. She always tried, but somehow the secret just slipped out.

'I'm going to dress up as a clown for the fancy dress party,' said her best friend Lucy. 'But don't tell anyone,' she added. 'It's a secret.'

''Course I won't tell anyone,' said Josie.

But when Kate said, 'Are you going to the fancy dress party?' Josie said right away, 'Oh yes! I'm going as a princess, and Lucy's going to be a clown.'

'That's funny,' said Kate. 'So am I. Mum's made me a special hat and some baggy trousers.'

'Fancy us both being clowns,' Kate said to Lucy when they met the next day. 'Isn't that funny!'

Lucy was very cross. 'It was supposed to be a secret.'

'Oh dear,' said Josie when Lucy told her what had

happened, 'I really did mean to keep the secret.'

Soon Josie's friends wouldn't share their secrets with her.

One day she found a group of friends giggling in a corner. 'What are you laughing about?' she asked.

'Oh, nothing. It's a secret,' said one.

'Tell me,' Josie begged. 'I won't breathe a word to anyone else.'

'Oh, you can't keep a secret,' said another, and they all laughed.

Josie felt a little bit shut out. 'I *can* keep a secret. I *can*,' she said.

'Oh no, you can't. You'd just tell everyone.'

'You wait,' said Josie firmly. 'I'll show you.'

One morning Josie arrived at school looking pleased with herself. 'I've got a very good secret,' she said, 'but I'm not going to tell anyone at all.'

'Go on,' said Kate. 'Tell us.'

'No.' Josie shook her head. 'I'm not telling anyone.'

Next day she was still smiling and she wouldn't say what the secret was.

By now Kate and Lucy were very curious.

'Is it something new to wear?' asked Lucy.

Josie shook her head.

'You're going on a visit, somewhere exciting,' said Kate.

'Wrong again.' Josie just smiled.

A few days later Josie said to her best friends, 'My

mum says I can ask you home to tea. Can you come on Friday?'

'Yes,' they both said eagerly, and they would ask at home if it was all right.

Lucy and Kate were very excited. Now they'd find out about Josie's secret.

After school on Friday they went home with Josie. When they went into her house by the front door, there was a large notice just inside. 'Secret this way' it said and there was an arrow.

'Follow me,' said Josie, 'and I'll show you the best secret ever.'

They went through the hall, through the living room and into the big kitchen.

And there Josie pointed to a cardboard box by the radiator.

'That's the secret,' she said proudly.

'Oh, look! Aren't they lovely!'

The two girls knelt down by the box where the family's brown and white spaniel lay happily with four wriggling brown and white pups beside her.

'That's the secret!' said Josie.

'If I'd been you,' said Lucy, 'I couldn't have kept them secret.'

'It was a really good secret,' said Kate.

And all her other friends agreed. It certainly was.

Shoes for Ted

I thought I'd give my shoes to Ted.
(They're nearly new and shiny red.)
I knew that he would not refuse
A pair of comfortable shoes,
But now I'll take them back because
They're miles too big for Teddy's paws!

Bumble our Puppy

When Bumble our puppy is out in the park,
He pulls at the lead and he's ready to bark
At flies and at bumble bees – why won't they stay?
As soon as he's near them, they're off and away!

Garden Fairies

Grown ups said that there weren't goblins in the garden.
They said that there weren't fairies there at all.
But Dolly and I know, that isn't really so,
For we saw them from the old stone wall.

They were hiding in the flowers, they were flying
   through the air,
We watched them and we smiled to see them
   play.
Then suddenly they vanished – I've no idea
   where.
I hope that they'll come back another day.

THE SHOEMAKER'S DAUGHTER

'What beautiful shoes!' everyone said.

Sam the shoemaker made all sorts of shoes – strong working boots, smart shoes for ladies, and the finest of dancing slippers. Sam loved his work, and he sang happily as he hammered and stitched.

One day a special messenger called at the shoemaker's workshop.

'The King's daughter is going to be married,' he told Sam. 'She has heard of your skill and wishes you to make her wedding slippers.'

He went on, 'They must be the very best slippers. Soft as silk, light as a feather, stitched with golden thread – and they must be ready in two weeks' time!'

'Then you must start right away, Father,' said Sam's daughter, Betsy.

Next day Sam began work on the golden slippers. He sang a little song as he tapped and stitched. He worked hard from morning to night, and at last the slippers were ready. Next day he would take them to the Palace and make sure they fitted the King's daughter.

That night he was very tired. He yawned as he locked up his workshop. Last of all, he looked at the golden slippers. They were the most beautiful shoes he had ever made.

Sam slept soundly that night, but when he woke in the morning, a dreadful thing had happened. The beautiful golden slippers had vanished!

'Oh dear! Oh, my goodness!' Poor Sam was quite distracted. 'I locked the door of the workshop. But some thief has got in! And the King's daughter is to be married in a few days' time – now she will go barefoot to her wedding!'

'Calm down, Father,' said his daughter, who was a sensible sort of girl. 'Eat your breakfast, and I will put on my thinking cap and try to decide what to do.'

So she thought long and hard. 'It wasn't a human thief,' she said. 'No human thief could have got through the locked door. And the window was open only a fraction. I know,' she said, 'I will go and ask the wise woman.'

Some people were afraid of the wise woman of the

village. But Betsy wasn't afraid of her, and she knew the old woman was very clever.

She went straight to the wise woman and told her the whole story. 'I must find the golden slippers,' she finished.

'Oh dear, what a to-do!' said the elves and other creatures swinging on the branches of the trees.

'Quiet!' ordered the wise woman. She leant on her stick, and closed her eyes and thought.

'You must go back home,' she told Betsy. 'When it begins to get dark, go down to the bottom of your garden, turn round three times, and you will see a toadstool. That's all,' she said suddenly and wouldn't tell Betsy anything more.

Betsy thanked her and went home again. She did exactly what the wise woman had told her. Yes, there was the toadstool, and sitting on the toadstool was a fairy. In the fairy's hand was one of the golden slippers.

'Oh, how beautiful!' said the fairy. 'Look!' she called to two fieldmice who were going shopping, 'Just look what fine shoes I have!'

'And they don't belong to you!' Betsy marched up to the fairy. 'You stole them! Give them back to me this minute.'

The fairy looked at Betsy in astonishment. 'Who are you?'

'I am the daughter of the shoemaker who made these golden slippers, which you stole,' said Betsy very loudly.

'Stole, indeed!' The fairy tossed her head.

'Yes you did,' insisted Betsy. 'My father made them specially for the King's daughter's wedding, and you have taken them.'

But the fairy wouldn't give them back.

Betsy tried everything. She tried shouting. The fairy just stopped her ears and refused to listen.

She tried coaxing. But the fairy just smiled and said, 'Finders keepers, losers weepers.'

Finally Betsy begged, 'Please, please give them back, or the King's daughter will go barefoot to her wedding and my father will be in such disgrace.'

'I don't care,' said the fairy.

Then Betsy thought of something else. 'Why don't you try them on?' she suggested.

'Oh yes,' said the fairy, 'why not?'

She put on the shoes and took a few steps. But immediately she fell over. 'Oh dear!' she wailed.

The rabbits and the mice laughed at her.

'They're much too big,' said the fairy crossly.

'Of course they are,' said Betsy. 'You look silly.'

The fairy didn't like the idea of looking silly. 'But I don't have any shoes,' she said, her mouth drooping.

'I have an idea,' said the shoemaker's daughter. 'Give

me back these slippers and I will ask my father to make you a pair all of your own.'

'Very well,' said the fairy, and she disappeared.

Thankfully Betsy snatched up the slippers and hurried back indoors.

Her father was overjoyed. He could hardly believe Betsy's story and he listened in astonishment as she told him, 'You must make a pair of fairy slippers.'

'Gladly,' said the shoemaker, and he mopped his brow.

So the King's daughter went to her wedding in the beautiful golden slippers, and the shoemaker started stitching once more. A few days later he had made another pair of slippers – light as silk, soft as a glove, but so tiny!

That night, as he locked the cottage door, he put the fairy slippers on the doorstep with a note, 'Please return if these slippers do not fit.'

In the morning the slippers and the note had gone.

Betsy never saw the fairy again, but she sometimes thought she heard music, and the lightest of dancing footsteps.

Mary, Mary, Quite Contrary

Mary, Mary, quite contrary,
How does your garden grow?
With silver bells and cockle shells
And pretty maids all in a row.

Pat-a-cake, Pat-a-cake

Pat-a-cake, pat-a-cake, baker's man!
Bake me a cake as fast as you can;
Pat it and prick it and mark it with B
And put it in the oven for Baby and me.

Bye Baby Bunting

Bye Baby Bunting
Daddy's gone a-hunting
To get a little rabbit skin
To wrap his Baby Bunting in.

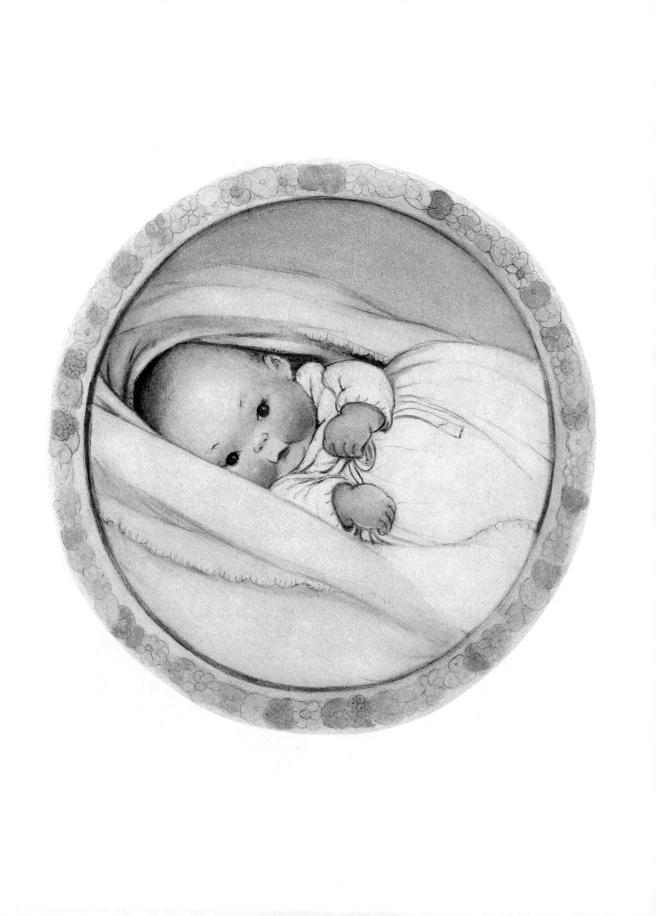

THE ROSE DOLL'S PARTY

'Saturday is a very special day,' said Mrs Mouse.
'Extra special,' said the elves.

'Mighty special,' agreed the rabbit.

'Why?' The dormouse woke up and rubbed his eyes.
'What's so special about Saturday?'

'Don't you know?' said Mrs Mouse.

'You really don't know?' said the rabbit.

'Just fancy not knowing!' said all the elves together.

'I'm still half asleep,' the dormouse yawned. 'But
please won't someone tell me – what is special about
Saturday?'

'It's the Rose Doll's birthday!' said the elves all
together.

'Of course!' said the dormouse. 'Fancy me forgetting!'

'So,' said Mrs Mouse, who was a busy sort of mouse,

'we must do something really special on Saturday.'

'A party,' said the dormouse at once, just to show that he was wide awake.

'Yes,' agreed the elves. 'A really good party.'

'A picnic,' said the rabbit, 'as it's summer time.'

They all patted him on the back and said, 'What a good idea!'

'I'll make fairy cakes and little biscuits,' said Mrs Mouse. 'And we'll write a proper invitation.'

So they wrote a little note to the Rose Doll and said 'Please come to a birthday picnic on Saturday. We will come and fetch you at eleven o'clock on the dot.'

Early on Saturday, Mrs Mouse, the elves, the rabbit, the dormouse and the other creatures, set off for the Rose Doll's house – a little thatched cottage on the edge of the wood.

'Funny,' said Mrs Mouse. 'The door is closed, and she doesn't seem to be about. Perhaps she isn't up yet.'

'But the sun's been up for hours,' said the rabbit.

'Let's ring the bell and see if she answers,' said one of the elves. So they pulled hard at the bell rope. The bell jangled loudly but there was no reply.

'Well, I'm going to look down the chimney,' said another of the elves.

Two elves climbed on to the roof, but they couldn't see down the chimney because a bird had built a nest on top.

Some of the others climbed a tree to have a better view, but there was nothing to see. Others peered in at the windows. 'No one at home!' they said.

'Oh dear,' said Mrs Mouse. 'Perhaps she's forgotten about the picnic – or perhaps she's gone away for the day.'

'Hallo, everyone! Am I late?'

It was the Rose Doll.

They all crowded round her. 'What happened? Did you forget?'

'Oh dear no,' the doll said. 'But you were all so kind asking me to a birthday picnic, that I wanted to bring some food. So I've been shopping. Look!' She opened her basket: it was full of bottles of lemonade, fruit and other good things to eat. 'I hope you'll share the food and eat it all up.'

They all cheered up then and set off for the wood. Mrs Mouse spread a checked tablecloth on the ground and everyone gathered round. They managed to eat all the sandwiches and cakes and biscuits and fruit, and drink the lemonade – because even very small creatures can eat and drink quite a lot, especially if there are a good many of them.

Afterwards the Rose Doll sat in the sunshine while all the little creatures danced round in a ring and sang, 'Happy Birthday to you.'

And because it was a special day, the dormouse stopped yawning and stayed awake long enough to join in the singing.

Knitting Needles

This scarf is for Grandpa – how pleased he will be!
I'm knitting in purl and in plain.
But keep dropping stitches. How silly of me!
I'll have to undo it again.

Us Three

There's Timmy who's older and going to be
tall,
And me in the middle, and Baby who's small,
We share out our toys and we don't fight at all,
It's ever such fun when there's three!

But whenever we're planning a prank or a game,
Whenever there's mischief they say I'm to blame,
Whatever the trouble it's always the same,
The one in the middle is me!

THE PATCHWORK QUILT

Sara had always wanted to sleep in the big bed at Gran's, under the patchwork quilt. And now was her chance – she was staying with Gran, all by herself, for two nights.

She snuggled down under the quilt, and Gran turned off the light. 'Sleep well,' she said.

But oh, it did seem strange. Sara tried very hard not to think of her little bed at home and the pretty blue curtains at the windows, and the pictures on the walls. And Mum and Dad just next door, and Smudge the puppy in his basket downstairs. Would he be missing her? Already Sara was feeling just a little homesick.

She tossed and turned in bed. Of course she wasn't lonely. Gran's room was just across the way and she had left the landing light on.

Sara tried and tried to go to sleep, but the more she tried, the more wide-awake she felt. She wasn't going to cry. After all, she was quite big.

It was no use. She sat bolt upright in bed, and a big tear rolled down her cheek. 'Oh dear!'

'All right?' said a voice, and there was Gran in her cosy pink dressing gown. 'Can't you sleep?'

'Er – no.' Sara didn't want to say she was homesick, but somehow Gran seemed to understand. She sat down on the bed.

'How do you like the patchwork quilt?' she asked.

'It's beautiful,' said Sara.

'I made it myself,' said Gran.

'Did you really?' Sara was quite interested.

'And what's more,' said Gran, 'every patch has a story.' She pointed to a patch of cotton material – green with a pattern of white and red flowers. 'That came from a dress your mum wore when she was a little girl. Oh, how I remember that dress! I made it for her when she was only six years old, to wear to her best friend's birthday party. She had bright green shoes to match, too. Well, on the day of the party it rained hard, and it started to rain again just as we left. Your mum was skipping along the path, trying to miss the puddles, because she didn't want to spoil her brand-new shoes, when – oops! – she tripped and fell right into a puddle. Her

66

new dress was all splashed with mud – what a sight she looked! We had to go home and change, I remember ...' Gran laughed.

'And this yellow material –' she pointed to another patch, 'this came from curtains in your mum's bedroom, when she was quite small. We were moving house and she didn't really want to go. She was going to miss the old house.'

'Fancy Mum being small,' said Sara, 'just like me.'

Gran nodded. 'Anyway, on the morning of the move, I took down the curtains from her bedroom, and as soon as we reached the new house I put them up again. And when she opened the bedroom door, there were her old curtains at the window, and teddy and polar bear and Daisy her favourite doll, all on the bed waiting for her.'

'So she didn't feel strange and new at all,' said Sara. 'These red patches,' she said, 'where did these come from?'

'They were curtains too,' said Gran. 'They had almost worn out but I didn't want to waste good material. And then there was a fancy dress party. Your mum wanted to go, and we couldn't think of a costume. Then I thought – why not a Spanish dancer? Your mum had dark hair and a fringe when she was little. So I made a red skirt out of the curtain material, and she had a black shawl that had belonged to *her* Gran, and a fan that Uncle

George had brought back from Japan. Oh, she did look nice . . .'

'And did she win a prize?' asked Sara.

'Yes, she did. When they all walked past the judges, your mum kept dancing and stamping her heels, just the way Auntie Josie had taught her, like a real Spanish dancer.'

'It's a story quilt really,' said Sara, 'and all about Mum.' She yawned. Funny, she was beginning to feel quite drowsy.

'I'll tell you the rest of the stories tomorrow night,' said Gran as she tucked Sara in.

Sara smiled. Somehow she didn't feel strange and homesick – not any more.

Won't You Share?

You've such a lot of apples there,
　You can't need three.
I'm feeling very hungry –
Won't you share just one with me?

Cheer Up!

Please don't be sad! Oh, do cheer up!
And smile again, says Patch the pup.
You're making me feel dismal too.
It's time we both stopped being blue.

Ready for the Rain

It was such a sunny day,
When I set out on my way,
And the sky was a clear, bright blue.
But when the sky turned black,
I'd my brolly and a mac,
Or I'd surely have been soaked right through.

MABEL
LUCIE
ATTWELL

THE HAPPY UMBRELLA

Hazel sang happily as she worked in the garden. It had been raining hard all morning, but now at last the clouds had blown away, the sun had come out and Hazel was enjoying being out in the open air, weeding among the flowers.

Suddenly she heard a small voice. 'Help me! Please help me!'

She turned round and could hardly believe what she saw. There was a small, cross-looking figure in a striped T-shirt and green trousers, carrying a bright green umbrella. He wore a peaked cap and had tiny wings on his shoulders. And that was the trouble. One of the wings had somehow got caught on a rose bush. The little creature tugged and tugged, but could not pull free.

'Hold on,' said Hazel. 'I'll help you.'

Gently she eased the wing this way and that, and in a moment the fairy was free.

'Oh!' The fairy shook his wings. 'I'm really most grateful. I don't know what I should have done. I might have been stuck here for ages, and I have an awful lot to do today,' he said importantly. He held out his little green umbrella to Hazel. 'Would you accept this as a thank-you present? One good turn deserves another, you know.'

'Why, thank you very much,' said Hazel, and before she could say more, the fairy had flown away. Hazel thought that it was a funny sort of present to give someone – after all, the sun was shining brightly now – but she put the umbrella away neatly inside the porch and went back outside.

The next morning it was pouring with rain again. Hazel decided to take her new umbrella and go into the village.

What a strange thing! As soon as she put up the umbrella, it seemed as if the sun were shining underneath. She felt so pleased and cheerful that she didn't mind the rain at all.

Just outside the village, Hazel met an old woman she knew. She was trudging along with no hat or umbrella to shield her from the rain and her thin coat was nearly soaked right through.

Almost before she knew what she was doing, Hazel was holding out her new green umbrella to the woman. 'Look,'

Hazel said, 'would you like to share my umbrella? I'm walking into the village too.' The old woman accepted gratefully, and they set off together down the road.

After they had gone only a few yards, the old lady found that she was as warm and as dry as toast. She felt as cheerful as if the sun were shining from a clear blue sky.

Outside the village shop were two men who were quarrelling bitterly. Everyone was staring at them.

Hazel had an idea. 'Excuse me,' she said to the two men, 'you are getting very wet standing there. Would you like to borrow my umbrella while I go into the shop?'

'That's kind of you, but no thank you,' said the first man.

'Don't be stupid,' said the second. 'That's just like you, always stubborn.'

'All right,' said the first, rather rudely, 'we'll take it.'

When Hazel and the old lady came out of the shop a few minutes later, the two men were laughing and joking, and not quarrelling at all. And what is more, the rain had stopped, and the sun was shining brightly between the parting clouds.

'What a fine present,' said Hazel to herself as she set off back home. 'This really is a happy umbrella!' After that, whenever it rained, she took the green umbrella with her. There was sure to be a use for it!

Up, Off and Away

It was far too hot in the kitchen
And 'twas such a beautiful day,
'We'll leave the oven and pots,' I said,
'And go for a holiday jaunt instead,'
So we flew up, off and away.

There was one little mouse,
Who belonged to the house,
And the kitchen fairies and me,
There's room for all on the rolling pin,
What fun we had on our merry spin
High over the sparkling sea!

My Little Brother

My little brother tripped and fell,
But then I hugged and kissed him well.
And in a very little while,
He dried his tears, began to smile.

THE LITTLE BOOS AT THE SEASIDE

There was such joy and excitement! Bunty and the Little Boos were going to the seaside – yes, really and truly. Grandpa had said so.

The Little Boos were so happy that they could hardly keep from jumping right up to the ceiling.

'But come, Boos,' said Bunty, in the middle of a wild dance round, 'we must get everything packed, or we'll never be ready in time.'

All the little creatures rushed backwards and forwards, fetching and carrying, collecting spades, pails, bats and nets. Nothing must be forgotten!'

'What a fuss,' grumbled Mops the dog. 'Just when I wanted to chase that cheeky cat next door.'

But no one took any notice of him!

At last everything was packed, and the Little Boos,

with shiny, clean faces, were gathered together with the luggage in the hall, waiting for the taxi to arrive and take them to the station.

But when the taxi driver arrived, and saw all the Boos, he said fiercely, 'I'm not taking insects. I never have taken insects, and I'm not going to start now.'

The King and all the Little Boos were very worried. It looked as if there would be no seaside for them after all.

They were all greatly relieved when Bunty came down the stairs.

'I'm not taking grasshoppers,' the taxi driver said.

'But they're not grasshoppers,' said Bunty sweetly. 'They're Little Boos, and this is the King. Look at his crown! You will take them, won't you?'

'Oh, all right then.' The driver grumbled a bit, but he took them, and off they went to catch the train.

It would take too long to describe all the wonderful things they saw as the train rushed through the country-side. Mops, in his desire to chase chickens, nearly fell out of the window when they were passing a farm, and the King would keep putting his head out of the window and nearly lost his crown.

But at last they all arrived safely, and rushed straight down to the sea.

'Hallo sea! We've arrived! We've arrived!' cried Bunty, waving her arms.

'We've arrived, we've arrived!' echoed the Boos in delight.

But Mops crept off up the beach. 'It's only a horrid great bath after all,' he said. 'Now I suppose they'll want to bath me!'

Bunty had promised to build the King a sandcastle all for himself. 'Kings always have castles,' she said.

So on the first morning, she set to work. All the Little Boos helped her. They rushed around bringing shells and pretty weeds and soon the castle grew tall.

But Mops had let an ugly little thought creep into his head. 'Why does Bunty build a castle for the King and not for me?' he thought. 'Everything is for the King. No one loves me or builds *me* things.'

When the castle was finished, the King stood bravely on the very top. All the Boos cheered, then they joined hands and danced round and round the castle.

Next morning, the King was up early and went down to the sea. A fisherman had just cast his line over the break-water and had gone off up the beach to have his breakfast.

Now the King had never seen a fishing-rod before, so he went up to have a look at it.

Suddenly he heard a little voice coming from the big basket nearby.

'Oh, please,' called the voice, 'please do let me out. I can hardly breathe. Oh, hurry, please!'

The King opened the lid and peeped in. There was a big fish huffing and panting.

'A good thing you have come,' said the fish. 'It was nearly too late.'

Then he told the King how he had got caught on the fisherman's line, and begged the King to help him into the sea.

The King soon helped the poor creature out of the basket and down to the water, and in two shakes of its tail, it had swum completely out of sight.

One day Bunty thought she would take the Little Boos on a picnic.

'We will take a boat,' she said, 'and row over to the Mermaids' Rock. Only be sure that none of you are left behind, for when the moon rises, the mermaids come up on that rock. They love little children – so much so that they always try to persuade any child they find to go down to their home below the sea. And remember this – if any child goes, he never comes back.'

The Boos all promised to be very careful, and soon they were climbing all over the rock and having a splendid picnic.

But the wicked Mops had heard what Bunty said, and he saw his chance for revenge.

Just when it was nearly time to go home, he persuaded the King to explore a little cave in the rock, just big enough for him to creep into.

When the little fellow was safely inside, Mops sat down outside and blocked up the hole, so that the King was a prisoner.

'Now,' said the wicked Mops, 'there you stop till the boat goes without you, and the moon rises and the mermaids come. They'll persuade you right enough, and you'll never bother me again!'

Soon Bunty's voice was heard calling, calling, and at last she had to go without them.

'Mops will swim home and bring the King on his back. It will be all right,' she said.

When the boat had quite disappeared, Mops let the King out.

'Now stay there and wait for the mermaids,' he barked as he plunged into the sea and made for home.

Poor little King, he was terribly worried, and it was lonely on that rock and quickly getting dark.

He called for Bunty to come to him, but there was no answer.

The moon came slowly out of the sea, and hardly had it risen than swish, swish, the King heard the sound of tails moving gently to and fro in the water.

'I'm not afraid,' said the King bravely. 'I needn't go if I don't want to.'

Presently the sweetest voice was heard singing from somewhere near the bottom of the rock:

MABEL
LUCIE
ATTWELL

Come away down, dear
Come away down.
Leave the green fields, dear,
Leave the grey town.
The sea hall is cool, dear,
And decked with white foam:
Oh, come away down, dear,
And make it your home.

The song came to an end and a beautiful little mermaid climbed on to the rock, and sat next to the King.

'You will come, won't you?' she whispered. 'I am a Princess, and you, I can see, are a King.'

But the little King shook his head. Bunty's words rang in his ears. 'And if a child goes, it never comes back.'

'Dear Princess,' he replied, 'I cannot come, for there is a little girl waiting for me over there,' and he told her his sad little tale of trouble.

'Then I will help you, King!' The little mermaid clapped her hands.

A large fish came swimming up. 'Take this King on your back, O Friend Fish,' she said, 'and carry him safely to Bunty.'

The King thanked her gratefully and was soon sailing away over the water.

'What a good thing you saved me this morning,' said

the fish presently, and the King saw that it was the creature he had rescued from the fisherman's basket.

'One good turn deserves another,' went on the fish. 'Hold tight now, here comes a wave!'

Meanwhile Bunty was very anxious, and she and the Little Boos sat patiently watching for the wanderers' return.

Soon a very wet and bedraggled Mops appeared.

'Where is the King?' they all cried.

'He has gone with the mermaids,' said Mops wickedly. 'He wouldn't come back.'

Bunty couldn't believe it. 'He'll come back, I know he will,' she sobbed. And they all waited and waited.

Then suddenly a speck appeared on the water. No! Yes! Yes, it *was* the King. 'Hurray! Hurray! Hurray!' they all cried.

And now comes the best part of the story. The King did not say a word about the cruel and naughty thing that Mops had done.

But the next morning, when a fierce crab hung on to Mops's tail and was pinching him cruelly, the King flew to the rescue, beating the creature off.

Then Mops's wicked thoughts all flew away, and he crept to the King's feet and begged to be forgiven.

And the King forgave him there and then.

Splashing

It's lovely weather for ducks, they say,
It's rained all night and it's rained all day.
We're splashing through puddles – what splendid
  fun!
It's lovely weather for everyone!

Daisy Chains

Daisy chains make Dolly's crown
And rings for either hand
A necklace for her favourite gown –
Oh, won't she just look grand!

THE VALENTINE FAIRY

Lindy was counting stitches when she felt the tug at the ball of wool. She was knitting a special birthday present for Dad – a pair of long socks to wear when he went out in cold weather. One, two, three, four, five, six, seven – 'Oh,' she said, as she felt another tug.

She looked down, and to her astonishment, there was a fairy sitting on top of her ball of wool. He was clearly a special sort of fairy, as he carried a bow and arrows. But although he had a round, rosy face, he didn't look at all happy.

'A-choo!' he sneezed. 'A-choo!'

'Have you got a cold?' asked Lindy.

'Yes, I should just think so,' said the fairy, sniffing. 'Here am I, supposed to be a St Valentine's Day fairy, I should be flying here and there, two days from now, bringing gifts and making people fall in love with each other. That's what happens when I'm around. But here I am shivering with cold, and not feeling a bit cheerful. No one wants a fairy around with such a dreadful cold.'

'Oh, dear,' said Lindy, but she didn't see what she could do to help.

She started counting stitches again. And then she had a very good idea. 'I'm sure you should be wearing something warm,' she said. 'Why don't you put on a jersey and a woolly hat and socks?'

'I haven't got any,' said the fairy sadly. 'You never saw a fairy in a woollen jersey and socks, now did you?'

'Well,' said Lindy, 'I think it would be much more sensible if you fairies dressed warmly, and then you wouldn't catch cold.' She went on, 'Listen! Come back in two days' time and I'll have something for you.'

The fairy sneezed again and flew away.

Lindy put down the sock, and got out some bright red wool. Then she began to knit, one plain, one purl.

She knitted a little red suit, and a pair of red socks, and finally, a little red woolly hat.

In two days' time the fairy arrived. Lindy could hear him coming. 'A-choo! A-choo!'

'How are you?' asked Lindy, for she was a kind girl.

'I've a code id by dose,' said the fairy.

'Well, these will keep you warm,' said Lindy, and she

handed him the little red suit, and the socks, and the woolly hat.

The fairy was delighted. 'Thank you!' he said, and dressed in his new clothes, he flew off.

All the other fairies gathered round him.

'You do look smart!'

'I wish I had a suit like that.'

When Lindy went to sleep that night, she thought she heard a voice singing a little song.

'I'm proud to boast

I'm as warm as toast,

No longer blue

And it's thanks to you.'

When she woke, she remembered the little song. It might have been a dream – or perhaps the fairy was just saying 'Thank you!'

I Sent a Letter to My Love

I sent a letter to my love
And on the way I dropped it.
One of you has picked it up
And put it in your pocket.

This Little Pig Went to Market

This little pig went to market;
This little pig stayed at home;
This little pig had roast beef;
This little pig had none;
This little pig cried, 'Wee, wee, wee!'
All the way home.

THE GENTLE DRAGON

Emily and her doll, Candy Mae, were playing in the garden. Emily was a little bored. It was very quiet because her best friend, Betsy, who lived next door, had gone to visit her Gran.

Then all of a sudden, Emily heard a strange sound. It sounded like someone crying. Who could it be?

And then, through the trees at the end of the garden, came a strange creature. Now Emily had lots of picture books and books of fairy tales, so she knew right away what it was.

'It's a dragon!' she said. 'Look, Candy Mae, a real live dragon!'

She wasn't a bit scared because she could see that the dragon wasn't fierce. It wasn't a very large dragon, and it was clearly upset about something because large tears rolled down its cheeks.

'Oh dear me!' it said. 'Oh dear! Oh dear!'

'Never mind,' said Emily, and she held out a handkerchief to the dragon so that it could dry its tears.

'Thank you,' said the dragon, and it stopped sobbing.

'Do tell me what's the matter,' said Emily.

'I'm no use as a dragon,' said the creature, its lip trembling. 'Dragons are supposed to be fierce and fight battles and so on. I never want to fight and I don't roar. The other dragons just laugh at me.' He gave a gentle roar.

'You see?' he said. 'That's the best I can do. Now that doesn't sound very fierce, does it?'

'No,' said Emily, 'I don't suppose it does.' She thought for a moment. 'Look – why don't you come and meet my friends? They'll cheer you up.' She led him into the house.

'Goodness!' said Mum. 'What's that?'

'It's a poor sad dragon,' said Emily, 'and I want him to meet my friends, so that he won't be sad any more.'

'Here they are!' she said. And there, sitting round the room were Emily's toys. There was old Ted and Brown Bear, the sailor doll and the scarecrow, a baby doll, and the wise old owl.

'Now,' said Emily, 'this is my friend the dragon and he's very sad because he's not fierce enough.'

'Bless my soul!' said the sailor doll.

'He seems a very fine dragon to me,' said the scarecrow.

The wise old owl didn't usually say much, for he slept all day and only woke up at night.

But suddenly he was wide awake.

'Why do you want to be fierce?' he asked.

'Because all the others are,' said the dragon with a sniff.

'I think,' said the owl, and they all waited to hear what he was going to say, 'I think you should be the only gentle dragon in the country . . .'

'Well,' said the dragon, 'that's not a bad idea.'

'You see,' said the wise old owl, 'people expect dragons to be fierce. They would get a great surprise when they found one who was quiet and gentle and helped people.'

'A very good idea!' said the dragon. 'I'll start now!'

'Hurray!' they all cried, and they waved the dragon off. He turned at the gate and gave a little gentle roar.

Long years afterwards, people told how a great dragon had been seen in the town. People shut their doors and locked them fast, but to their astonishment, the dragon turned out to be very quiet.

It helped by puffing on days when there was no wind, so that the washing dried. It sat around for hours so that visitors could draw its picture. And you often heard it singing a happy little song.

Emily heard the stories and she smiled. She knew it was her dragon.

The Photographer

Let me take your picture, please!
Do stand still and all say 'Cheese'.
I'm an expert – soon you'll see
What a picture this will be!

Teatime

Is anyone in? I've come for tea.
Look at the treats I've brought with me!
Fresh baked scones and a pot of jam.
Are you hungry? I'm sure I am!

Busy Day

Goodness, what a day it's been,
Making sure the house is clean.
Hustling, bustling here and there,
Sweeping, cleaning everywhere.

THE CHRISTMAS ROBIN

How cold it was! People drew the curtains and gathered round the fireside. 'We'll have a white Christmas this year, that's certain,' said the old people.

All the children were very excited.

'A white Christmas!' said Clare.

'Sledging and building snowmen!' said Thomas.

Then one night it snowed. The children woke up in the morning to find the whole garden covered with a soft downy blanket of white.

'We mustn't forget the birds,' said Clare, as she watched a robin hopping cheerfully around the back doorstep.

So she went out and scattered crumbs for the birds. She put out water too, and she and Thomas hung a bag of nuts on a branch of the old pear tree. And every day the robin came to the back door.

Clare told her friends about feeding the birds in winter, so other children put out crumbs and fat and nuts and other scraps. They fed the birds every day and watched as robins and sparrows and blackbirds swooped down to eat.

Soon it would be Christmas. Thomas and Clare started to make paper chains and silver stars and decorations for the tree.

'But,' said their mother, 'we don't have holly or greenery. Holly with bright red berries – that's what we need.'

'Getting ready for Christmas then?' Clare and Thomas and their little sister Sally were shopping with their mother in the village, when they met the farmer's wife. She smiled at the children.

'Now don't forget,' she said, 'if you want some holly, you're welcome to go through our wood.'

The children's mother thanked her. 'That's splendid,' she said. 'We'll go tomorrow.' And Clare made up her mind that she would draw a very special Christmas card for the farmer and his wife.

Next day the children wrapped up warmly with boots and woolly hats and scarves, and set out with their mother towards the wood. 'Look at my footprints!' cried Thomas, taking giant strides along the path, and pointing to the tracks in the snow.

Then suddenly there was a chirping.

'It's like a robin singing,' said the children's mother. 'Yes, look, it's a Christmas robin.'

'It's singing, "Follow me, follow me",' said Clare.

'Well, maybe it is,' their mother laughed.

They rounded a curve in the path and there was a holly tree covered with bright red berries – just what they wanted.

But only the children noticed something else – the mice and elves and woodland creatures who scurried along the path. Clare tried to tell her mother, but as soon as she said, 'Oh, look!' they seemed to vanish.

'I can't see anything,' said her mother, but there was a rustling in the undergrowth and Clare knew the little creatures had scampered for cover in case they were seen.

On they went, carrying bunches of holly, until the path widened. 'Follow, follow,' Clare was sure the robin was chirping.

And now they came out into a little clearing in the wood. Everyone gasped – for there stood a splendid snowman.

He had an old felt hat on his head and a red and white striped muffler round his neck. There were two long sticks for his arms, and at the end of the sticks a

pair of old leather gloves. He had stones for his eyes and mouth, and a pipe in his mouth. He looked as if he were smiling.

Sally stood and gazed at him. 'Hallo, Mr Snowman!' she said.

'Who would build a snowman here? That's a mystery,' said the children's mother.

Around the snowman's feet were snowballs – but only the children could see the mice and the elves clambering on top of them. And only the children could hear the squeaks of excitement.

The wise old owl looked out of a hole in the tree, and nodded. 'More snow on the way,' he said, 'that's for sure.'

And suddenly Clare heard the robin chirping again. 'Thank you very much,' it seemed to be saying. And Clare thought perhaps this was its way of saying 'thank you' for the food and water in the harsh winter weather.

'Time to go home,' said the children's mother, so off they went home, along the path towards the village.

'I wonder who built that snowman?' said the children's mother later on. 'What a lovely surprise!'

Snuggling down in bed later on, Clare thought about the robin. She was quite sure it was the robin who came every day to the back door. And was it really saying 'thank you'? Well, perhaps it was!

We Wish You a Merry Christmas

We wish you a merry Christmas
We wish you a merry Christmas
We wish you a merry Christmas
And a happy New Year.

MABEL
© LUCIE
ATTWELL

To Bed, To Bed

'To bed, to bed,' said Sleepyhead;
'Let's wait awhile,' said Slow;
'Put on the pan,' said Greedy Nan,
'Let's sup before we go.'

Sleeptime

Fast asleep and snug abed,
Goodnight, little sleepyhead.
Now the toys are put away,
It's time to dream of yesterday.

And what will morning bring to you?
A whole new day with lots to do.
So sleep in peace, in slumber sound,
Until the busy day comes round.